Rainbow

D0536667

Abdullah turned over yet again in his bed. He was finding it hard to close his eyes. Normally he would have fallen fast asleep by now. It had been two hours since he had offered his *fajr* prayer. But today he could not sleep. He was nervous.

He quickly turned the alarm off, on his Mosque-shaped adhan clock, the second it came on. It was going to be a big day today. It was his first day at his new school.

His family had just moved from Ashfield, a small town in the north of England. He had heard a lot about the city of Astonborough and how big it was, with thousands of people, all in a hurry, rushing around. Although Abdullah had asked many of his friends why everyone seemed to be in such a hurry, no one had actually given him a good enough answer. He could still remember Ahmad, a thin boy at his old school telling him, "Be careful Abdullah and stick to your own." Abdullah wasn't sure what Ahmad had meant.

Abdullah entered the large, colourful playground of Rainbow Junior School. There were hundreds of children all making lots of noise. He could not help noticing that the playground was full of white faces, except one black boy who was sitting all by himself near the large, rainbow-coloured school gates. The gates were quite remarkable. Abdullah couldn't help admiring them. They said the name of the school with each letter in a different colour of the rainbow.

R was in red, A was in orange, I in yellow and so on, going all through the colours of the rainbow. He thought it was quite clever. However, it was not as clever as his Auntie Munirah who had shown him how to remember the colours of the rainbow in a beautiful rhyme she had made up.

"Well, children..." he could remember his
auntie saying, "the easiest way to remember the
colours of the rainbow is to sing this song:

Red and yellow and pink and green,
You are a Muslim; Islam is your din,
Don't forget purple, orange and blue,
The colour of Islam is the colour of you."

Abdullah was quite impressed with Auntie
Munirah at the time. "Er... I thought it was
something to do with Richard of York," said
Ibrahim, Abdullah's cousin, interrupting her.

"Well, don't you think this is a lot easier to

remember and makes more sense?" asked Auntie Munirah. All the children nodded their heads in agreement.

Abdullah walked towards the brightly-coloured climbing frames. He was missing his old school and his old friends. Memories of the things they used to do together suddenly came rushing to his mind. He could remember the old den, hidden in a corner of the old park, which he and his friends, Baby and Bablu, had built from an old mattress and bits of scrap wood. They would get together,

everyday after school, in their secret den and all
three friends would promise each other that they
would stay friends forever and treat each other like
brothers. Bablu would start by putting his hand
out in front of him. Then Abdullah would put his
hand over Bablu's and finally Baby would put his
hand on top of Abdullah's hand and they would
hold still for a few seconds while they sang their
secret brotherhood promise:

Brothers forever, brothers forever,
Through sunshine and bad weather,
Wherever we go we shall be together,
Brothers forever brothers forever.

They would repeat this three times and then,

after saying *Assalamu 'Alaicum* to each other, they would leave the den for that day, without saying another word.

Baby was the eldest of the three but looked the youngest. That's why everyone called him Baby, for he never seemed to get any older. Bablu was the youngest but also the smartest and in Abdullah's eyes he was the best den maker in the whole world.

CHAPTER TWO
The Bullies

Abdullah was walking towards the climbing frames, lost in his own thoughts, when suddenly his thoughts were interrupted by a loud voice calling from behind. "Hey blackie!" the voice shouted. Abdullah turned around to see a group of three white boys staring at him, all about his age but bigger than him in size. They looked very rough.

"We're talking to you coloured boy!" one of
the boys shouted. Abdullah started to walk away
slowly from the group. He did not know what
to say to them. It wasn't that he was scared of
them, no not at all. He wasn't a chicken. No, in
fact Abdullah could remember his dad, clearly
saying to him "Abdullah, one lion is better than a
thousand sheep." Abdullah had always believed
that he was a lion but he did not want to make
trouble. He knew that fighting would not solve the
problem.

"Scared are you?" a different voice called

laughingly from behind. "Well you'd better be."

All of a sudden the school bell rang. Abdullah made his way to his new class, leaving the group of boys behind him in the playground. As he entered his new classroom he couldn't help noticing the smell. It reminded him of his old school back in Ashfield. He loved the smell at his old school. It smelt of books and ink. He loved books. He loved to read. He could read all day long.

Abdullah sat down at his new desk. He looked over his shoulder to find to his surprise that the group of bad boys, he had seen earlier in the playground, were sitting right behind him in his class. He promised himself that he would ignore them completely. He remembered his mum telling him, while she was packing his school lunch this morning, "Remember, Abdullah, people can call you all sorts of bad names but a person is good or bad only in the sight of Allah."

CHAPTER THREE
Mrs Tickledum's New Class

Abdullah looked towards the blackboard at his new teacher.

"Welcome everyone to Rainbow Juniors," said Mrs Tickledum with a wide smile on her face. She seemed to be in a very jolly mood. "As you will all know our school is a shining example for the whole city. Yes, we are proud that our school

welcomes pupils from all backgrounds, colours
and races," said the teacher in a funny sort of way,
almost giggling as she spoke.

Abdullah started to feel a little nervous, for it
seemed that the whole class, and especially the
gang of boys, were all staring at him. After all, he
was the only pupil who was of a different colour
in the room. He noticed a small boy at the back
of the classroom who was not looking at him, but
everyone else seemed to have his or her eyes fixed
on Abdullah.

"Rainbow School is not just a rainbow in
name," the teacher went on "but we are truly

open to embrace people of all colours." There was
a little noise from the crowd at the back, but they
soon quietened down.

It didn't seem to be much of a rainbow with
only three colours, Abdullah couldn't help
thinking to himself. After all, there was just
himself and the other black boy he had seen in the
playground; everyone else seemed to be white in
colour.

After that, morning lessons went well, Abdullah
tried to keep himself out of the gang's way, and
soon the bell rang for dinner.

CHAPTER FOUR
The Colour-blind Boy

Abdullah sat down on his own, at a table in the school dining hall.

"Can we have some of your curry?" the biggest of the boys said, as the group of bullies made themselves comfortable at the table where Abdullah was eating. "I'm sorry," Abdullah replied politely, "I don't have any. I only have two sandwiches and an apple. If you want to share them, you can." Abdullah actually thought that their mothers had forgotten to put a lunch box in their school bags this morning.

"What, no curry?" said the same rough voice. "My dad says that's only thing you lot eat."

"Leave him alone," another voice interrupted suddenly from a table close by.

Abdullah looked over at the table. It was the small boy Abdullah recognised from the morning class. The only one who had not stared at him. He was also white like the group but he seemed different; he was too cool for a ten-year-old.

"He hasn't done anything to you, has he?" the cool boy said very confidently to the group of bullies. "Now leave him alone," he added.

The cool boy wasn't big or anything but Abdullah could tell that the group of boys were somehow affected by his words. He seemed to have a charm about him, a kind of warmth that only few people have.

"But Adam, he's not like one of us, er… you know, he's not our colour, is he? I mean he's a… " The big boy's stuttering was interrupted by Adam who got up suddenly and walked towards the group with a cool sort of walk.

"He's what?" Adam said, in his usual cool way, staring at the leader of the pack, the big boy who was doing all the talking. "I can't tell the difference between him and us in colour, can you?" Adam the cool boy said with a questioning look on his face.

The boys didn't say a word. They dared not. Not that they were scared of him, but because they had a kind of respect for him. In fact the whole school did, even the teachers. It was his strong character and his cool way of doing things that made people take him seriously. He never seemed to get angry. "But then

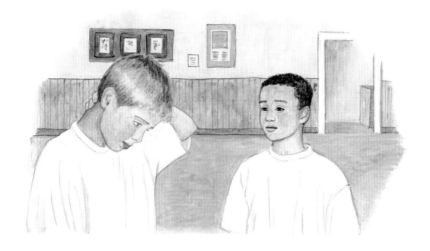

again, I am colour blind," Adam said, turning his head away from the big boy.

A sort of confused smile appeared on the face of the leader of the boys. "You're not really colour-blind are you… are you?" he said, trying to make eye contact with Adam.

"OK, I'm not, but maybe I choose to be. Maybe I choose not to see what colour other people are," Adam said sounding a lot older. "After all, your skin colour doesn't make you a better person, does it?" he added, facing towards the gang again.

The big bully's face had turned slightly paler by now and he was looking slightly down at the floor as if he was showing some sort of guilt. He looked up at Adam quickly and with a slight nod of his head walked off, with the other two boys following him.

Abdullah was beginning to like Adam more and more by the minute. He liked how cool Adam was and how everyone had so much respect for him and, most of all, of how he had stuck up for Abdullah when he needed a friend. He knew that's what really counted.

CHAPTER FIVE
Friendship Begins

As soon as the gang of bullies had left, Adam,
the cool boy, put out his hand for Abdullah to
shake. *"Assalamu 'Alaicum,"* he said.

Abdullah seemed to be in a sort of shock. He
waited for a second and then muttered with a
shaky voice, "er… are you er… a Muslim?"

"Of course, *Al-Hamdulillah,"* Adam said pleased,
with a smile on his face.

"But … er I thought you were… I mean you are…" Abdullah wasn't sure how to say it. Abdullah had never seen a white Muslim before. All the Muslims he knew were brown, except Yusuf, a black boy who had lived on his street a few doors away. It wasn't that he was racist or anything but it was just that nobody had told him about these things. In a funny sort of way he felt a little like the big boy and his gang who had been saying nasty things to him. Maybe they hadn't been told anything different by their mum or dad either. Abdullah's mind was full of questions.

"So who is being racist now?" said Adam with a warm friendly face. "Can't white people be Muslims? I think you should also choose to be colour-blind, Abdullah," said Adam.

"You're right. I'm sorry, Adam," said Abdullah feeling really silly about what he had just said. "It's just that I have never come across this before and no one has ever told me that Islam was for people of all colours. I know it sounds silly but I always thought it was for us, you know… er… brown people."

"It's OK, brother," Adam said in his usual cool style.

Abdullah took Adam's hand and shook it, and then he gave Adam a big hug.

"And thanks for helping me," Abdullah said with tears in his eyes.

"No problem. That's what brothers are for," Adam said in his cool voice.

"If only everyone was colour-blind like you," Abdullah said, handing one of his sandwiches to Adam.

As time passed by, Adam and Abdullah became best friends. They started hanging around with each other even after school. They found out that they didn't live very far away from each other, which was even better. Adam invited Abdullah to his house. Abdullah was excited. Adam's mother and father were new to Islam and hadn't been Muslims for long and Abdullah could see that Islam was stronger in their hearts than he had seen in many people who were born as Muslims.

Adam got to know Mrs Tickledum quite well too. In fact she had a sister who lived in Ashfield. Adam had learnt that it's hard to judge someone without actually getting to know them properly first. Sometimes it takes time to get to know someone and some people are a lot nicer than we first think they are.

"So when are you going to invite me to your house?" Adam said to Abdullah one day, while they were sitting on the swings in the local park.

"Er, soon, *Insha' Allah*" Abdullah said nervously. "Yes, very soon," he added. He didn't know what to say to Adam. He knew that even though his family were born Muslims, they still hadn't reached being colour-blind like Adam's family, or at least that's what he thought. He could picture his dad shouting at him as he walked through the door with Adam: "Who is this *gora* (white boy) and what have I told you about hanging around with white people?" Even though he had never heard these words from his own dad he definitely had heard them from other dads. He wasn't sure how to say it. He would have to some day, so why not today, he thought to himself.

Later on that evening Abdullah approached his dad. *"Abbu,"* Abdullah said shaking. "I want to tell you something." He started to build up his courage.

"Go ahead, son, I'm listening." His dad folded up the evening newspaper and looked at Abdullah.

"Well, er, I was wondering if I could invite a friend over," Abdullah said bravely.

"Yes, why not?" his dad replied.

"But he's… I mean, he's…" Abdullah started to struggle to get the right words out of his mouth.

"He's what?" his dad said, starting to look worried.

It was hard for the words to come out but Abdullah knew he had to say them.

"He's white," Abdullah said quickly so as to get it over and done with, waiting for his dad to shout at him now, any second.

"And so?" his dad said in a questioning tone.

" Er… nothing," Abdullah said, surprised.

"Well then, call him over," his dad carried on. 'Does he have parents by the way?"

"Yes he does and they are Muslims too. They are

very nice. I have met them." Abdullah said, beaming with excitement.

"Well, what are we waiting for then? Let's call them all over for dinner," his dad said, also excited now.

The next evening Adam and his family arrived at Abdullah's house. They talked about almost everything. It was a very nice atmosphere. The two families got to know each other quite well.

As everyone busily chatted away, there was a knock at the door. Abdullah's dad went to answer it. A few minutes later he walked in with a whole load of people behind him.

Abdullah was trying to make out who it was but he was finding it difficult to see through all the people.

"Look who's come all the way from Ashfield to pay you a visit Abdullah," Abdullah's dad said, as he stood at the door hiding the guests behind him.

Abdullah could not believe his eyes; it was Baby and Bablu, his best friends from his old school along with their families. They had come all the way from Ashfield to stay with Abdullah for the half term holidays.

Bablu put his hand out in front of him. Abdullah put his hand over Bablu's. Baby then put his hand over Abdullah's.

"Wait," said Abdullah. Baby and Bablu looked shocked. Maybe Abdullah had forgotten them, they thought to themselves.

Abdullah called Adam. Adam came over and put his hand in between Abdullah's and Baby's.

Baby and Bablu smiled again. "Now we can say it," said Abdullah. "We are four now, not three," he added looking at Adam. Then the four friends sang their secret brotherhood promise:

Brothers forever, brothers forever,
Through sunshine and bad weather,
Wherever we go, we shall be together,
Brothers forever, brothers forever.

As Adam and his family were about to leave that evening, Adam's dad gave something to Abdullah's dad. It was a gift. Abdullah's father opened it quickly after saying *Jazak-Allah Khair*. It was a beautiful copy of the Holy Qur'an, covered in a soft green leather pouch.

"I'm sorry, I didn't know which colour you like," said Adam's dad.

"It's alright," Abdullah's dad replied, looking at Adam and Abdullah with a big smile, "I'm colour-blind."

They all laughed.